Broken Shells
of
Memories

Gladstone

Cover Image by Emi Young

To the memory of my parents

Acknowledgment

To my wife Yuki and my children Emi and Kyle; without their support and patience this book would never have been completed.

Contents

Introduction

"And once the storm is over, you won't remember how you made it through, how you managed to survive. You won't even be sure, whether the storm is really over. But one thing is certain. When you come out of the storm, you won't be the same person who walked in. That's what this storm's all about."

Haruki Murakami, *Kafka on the Shore*

"There's always something one's ignorant of about anyone, however well one knows them; and that may be something of the greatest importance."

T. S. Eliot, *The Confidential Clerk*

I wander
an empty beach
lost
in broken shells
of memories
while heartless gulls
screech in disdain

Broken Shells of Memories

Abandoned
places still exist
Immured within
Ruins
of a time
long departed

Desolate swing
in the night
calling out
Wind chime
of tears

Broken Shells of Memories

A child chasing leaves
the wind pulls away
Will you ever love me?

Under the shadow
of a dead tree
a young pine struggles

Broken Shells of Memories

The young boy
left his room and
with the quietest of steps
crept down the hall
to the living room
All he wanted
was a sign
from the man who sat
engrossed
in his newspaper

"Dad?"

The man
folded his paper
turned his head
Their eyes met
He felt the man
looking down on him

*"I don't think I should
kiss you goodnight anymore
It's not that I don't love you
I just think I'm too old now."*

He would never forget
the unexpected collision
of pride and sadness
caught in
the man's eyes
that evening

He was always probed with
Why do you
think that way?
It took years
before he thought to question
Why don't they
think this way?

Broken Shells of Memories

There are memories
I wish would disappear
Not from the past
but these moments
here with you now

Gladstone

I was always the last leaf
nobly hanging on
hoping someone
would notice
embrace me as their hero
But they always chose
the fallen ones
the bright
the colourful
to press and preserve
in their hearts

Broken Shells of Memories

I have long wrestled
with a yearning
to belong
to fit in
Yet, I remain deaf
to the siren's song
and untouched
by the lotus's allure
I am left with the notion
that there is something wrong
with me

He became a papier-mache
Every incident stuck upon
an earlier one
Torn strips of life
overlaid and dried out
fabricated upon a form
devoid of function and merit
He endured
clad in rags
tailored by the entirety
of his experiences

Broken Shells of Memories

He wanted
to tell
her how
he felt
but he was afraid
Not of going
forward
but of losing
what they had

Watching transfixed
in melancholic enchantment
as flakes of snow
feathered down
kissed her eyelids
her cheeks
her lips
then vanished into her
as he had longed to do
but knew he never would

Broken Shells of Memories

I will never know your love
and you will never know
how early and long
I have loved you
Bitter consolation
watching our breath clouds
embrace and become one
on this cold
and brittle morning
of farewell

He trusted her
she was
the first person
who
when she said
I love you
he believed
Because of her
he began to accept
that he could be
worthy of love
from others
and from himself

With a tear
love vanished
The kiss of a raindrop
upon a skeleton flower

I throw things
at you
to keep you
from noticing
the cracks
in my walls

Broken Shells of Memories

By the time
I had fallen
back to earth
you had stolen
her away

Alone here
looking at the stars
I can see your eyes
but I know
you cannot see mine
you are looking at his

Night and day
in your embrace
he will lie

His hand whispers
across your body
dusting away
fingerprints
Sweeping off all traces
of the one who was
there before

Lambent stars
a billion miles away
closer to me than you

He wanted her
to hurt
as she had
hurt him
No,
worse
He wanted her
to feel guilty
anything just
to hold her again

Broken Shells of Memories

There were footprints facing him
which led off into the night
As the snow began to fall
they became less discernible
A bilious panic consumed him
Dropping to his knees
he brushed at the snow with his hands
in desperation, trying
to preserve any evidence
that she had been there
He realized too late
that his efforts
more than the falling snow
were destroying the final traces of her
He knelt there
more numb than cold
Everything he ever tried to do
it seemed
only made things worse

Without you
the echo
from a drop
of rain

Broken Shells of Memories

No longer plagued
with the bitterness
of knowing
that he
now occupies
the space
in your arms
I sufferer only
the desolation
of not being
there myself

When you left
I vowed
to always love you
It was meant
as a romantic attestation
But after nights alone
innumerable
I realized
that it was
a curse

Broken Shells of Memories

A photograph of you
on the shores
of Lake Ontario
counting geese
wearing the sweater
knitted for me
by my mother
Your cards and letters
and a book of short fiction
A gift from you
with a handwritten
note on the inside cover
"with all my love
and admiration
and my last 20 dollars
may you enjoy this book
as much as I enjoy you!"
And my ring
which you wore
on a chain
around your neck
Flotsam and jetsam
of a shipwrecked love
Castaways on an island
called *Memories*

Photographs
intoxicated with memories
cannot bring you here
They only accentuate
the distance

Broken Shells of Memories

Another futile jaunt
to the post box
Empty
Mirroring his hopes
It had been more than
a few weeks
Still no reply
An ancient sailing ship
could have crossed
the Atlantic
and returned by now
He mused
She was but 350 miles
distant
It felt like more
What did the silence mean?
He tried
to read between the lines
But in the absence of a letter
he could not perceive
the lines to read between

Dry ink on paper
Letters unsent
The face of a girl
struggles to free itself
from the snares
that bind to memories
Diminishing like a slow
contracting pupil

Broken Shells of Memories

It was only afterwards
he came to realize
that had he not lost her
he might never
have found
who he could be

If not for her
he would not
have come to know
that he had the capacity
to extend love
Not just to others
but to himself

There are times
when a tear
is the only means
of releasing
what has long been
confined

Is it the end
of winter
or the beginning
of spring?
That peculiar
dwelling
when coldness
begins to melt
and crocuses
break through
When you are still
unconvinced
that it is over
Thoughts lost within
the ticking of the clock
The sun yawns
through the blinds
generating hope
but not much warmth
Rays stretch
across the countertop
to the mug that
loiters there forsaken
Inside a layer of dust
slumbers
as memories languish

Broken Shells of Memories

You packed your suitcases
with all that belonged to you
and it was done
Lately,
I have been wondering
after all this time
would it be possible that
you might still have my heart
somewhere in your possession?
Within a cabinet gathering dust
Perhaps in a musty shoebox
along with old photographs
cobwebbed in the attic
Or was it tossed out
during a spring cleaning
A garage sale offering
pawed over and rejected
abandoned at the end of the drive
in a half crushed cardboard box
with all the other refuse
that no longer belongs

Forenoon
Upon the meadow
Dew still lingers
Your kiss, my lips

Broken Shells of Memories

Eventide
As moonflowers awaken
fireflies simulate
the glister of your eyes
and a woodland stream
mimics your laughter

The perfect conversation
You curled in me
Lost in the fire
No words spoken

She liked walking
he enjoyed a walk
Subsequently
they would never
be in step

It was made
clear to him
the dust on the floor
was more deserving
than the thoughts
in his head

Even
with you
I am alone

It began well enough
Setting out
naively optimistic
under a morning's red sky
Not long in
the weather changed
A pall of all-embracing
greyness descended
Grim dark ragged
clouds crept
across the landscape
A soundless sullen fog
of Cimmerian darkness
shrouded their world
White squalls swept
across the road
like sidewinder snakes
racing over sand
A thousand arrows
of sleet and graupel
hailed relentlessly
Wiper blades toiled
like galley slaves
It was impossible to see
what was ahead
He held tight
to the wheel
straining to keep them
on the road
The storm was unremitting
The longer they travelled
the greater the intensity
Everything became
more frigid and icy

Broken Shells of Memories

Thinking purblind
it would be without incident
Now he just wanted it to end
There seemed no escape
no respite
no way out
Vicious angry gusts
battered his mind
wore him down
until he himself was cold and frigid
Despair began to whisper
How much longer could they go on?
The wind cursed violently
in response
He fought hard
to stay
in control
It seemed that conditions
kept worsening
He caught sight of
a snow-encrusted
roadside mailbox
that marked
the turning point
They spun down the lane
Hope pressed hard
on the accelerator
ploughing into the endless
waves of snowdrifts
But it was not enough
Overwhelmed they stalled out
under the sardonic grin
of the storm
Drained and exhausted

he leaned back
head throbbing
jaw locked
They sat silent
Alone together
within a raging tempest
He glanced in her direction
She was vacantly staring
through the blizzard
towards the dark image
of a house barely visible
past the bleakness
Neither had said much
since it began
They needed to move on
get out
from where they were
She had not brought a coat
She never listened!
He reached over
to the back seat
grabbed his overcoat
and surrendered
it to her
Without a word
She abandoned him
for the distant dark
shadow of home
He watched her
as she struggled
to make her way
Staggering stumbling
with each step
through deep troughs

Broken Shells of Memories

He should have gone with her
He closed his eyes
lost within
the howl of wind
snow and freezing rain
His eyes opened
to find himself alone
in blackness
bitterly cold throughout
How long had it been?
Only silence and gloom
greeted him
when he entered the house
He tripped and fell
on his overcoat
lying damp and discarded
in a heap upon the floor
Warily he continued
to make his way
to the bedroom
A solitary lamp
on the bedside table
emitted just enough light
to reveal her curled up
cocooned in blankets
He avoided the bed
shuffled over
to a barren wooden chair
hiding in a darkened corner
He slumped down
elbows upon knees
head cradled in hands
She no longer loved him
He urgently needed to believe

she still did
He wanted to love her too
but there was remoteness now
Few words were exchanged
despite the need
Conversations reduced
to minimalist utterances
of the mundane
Visiting his thoughts
was a place
she was unable
or unwilling to go to
Her deafness to him
had caused him to
become mute
He waited until convinced
she was asleep
Then he spoke to her
through the gloom
across the distance
Giving voice to everything
he could not say
yesterday
today
tomorrow
until his face was wet
and his soul dry
The room had quietened
the storm having abated
He sat there
listening to the hush
of her sleeping breath
The sound and rhythm
had a soporific effect

Broken Shells of Memories

After some moments
he left the darkness
crossed the empty space
crawled in the bed
He held her
like he wanted her
to hold him
like she used to
Before the weather changed
Before the storm

I want to go back
to before
sides of the bed
became demarcated
and conversations
turned into minefields

Broken Shells of Memories

They exited the vehicle
surveyed the grounds
Chattering like excited squirrels
they moved on to examine
the lodgings
Finally left to himself
he drank in the quietness
Nothing save the sound
of autumn leaves tobogganing
down through the trees

Gladstone

I wondered all morning
at the sound of a leaf
striking my window

Do autumn leaves
long to be buds again
in the moments
before they fall?

Let passion consume
the merest breath
within an instant
Too soon magnolia petals
begin their migration
to soil

Broken Shells of Memories

Walking through the old neighbourhood
All that once was familiar has disappeared
My compass spins; no North Star to guide
Why do the footprints of progress
necessitate wiping off
all fingerprints of my youth?
I sail into evening rudderless and lost

When I was a young,
I remember people saving money,
getting their passports stamped,
traveling the world and saying
"Wow! Look at that, look at that!"
Now, so many people save up their money,
travel downtown,
get their bodies stamped and say
"Wow! Look at me, look at me!"

Broken Shells of Memories

It is a shame
to realize only now
that I was most happy
when I had nothing
but a run-down apartment
barely enough to eat
a bottle of cheap wine
and nights entwined
in your arms
on a futon mattress

Life's journey
fraught with cruel irony
when you realize
years later
how another's
love for you
could have changed
your life
in all the ways you needed
but you were unable
to understand that
until you had travelled
the roads and paths
that led you to now
the moment when
you comprehend
what accepting their love
would have meant
but now
is too late

Broken Shells of Memories

He had been adrift
for some time
Assailed by a
harrowing angst
He sojourned
deep into the forest
intent on
extricating himself
from the wasteland
he was lost in
He secured an austere Bunkie
within some woodlands
He stood silent
on the small, covered deck
attached to the main cabin
His mind absorbed
in the surroundings
A sombre palette
of feuillemorte
charcoal grey and shades
of earthen brown
blotted out the understory
He was most struck by
the vibrant
emerald, green moss
which embraced
all manner of
snags, stumps, logs
and rocks
without prejudice
The gentle psithurism
of trees encouraged him
to listen within the quiet
He spent the last few days

foraging
the landscape
of his mind
Thoughts trailing off
pawing and sniffing
everything encountered
along the way
A shudder of wind
sent leaves spiraling down
Each one a unique snapshot
of the life of a tree
They formed a collage
of leaf litter reminiscences
upon the forest floor
In their midst sat several
moss covered rocks
Islands of tranquility
in a sea of orphaned memories
The spasmodic
sputtering of the kettle
interrupted his reverie
He switched off the gas
and tilted the kettle over
a large earthenware mug
The steaming water
dove in and swam with
the overly generous measure
of spiced rum already there
awaiting companionship
He withdrew to
an old Muskoka chair
in the corner of the deck
Clasping the mug
snuggly in both hands

Broken Shells of Memories

welcoming its warmth
He rested his eyes
and listened through the quiet
It began to mizzle
The sound of droplets
on the corrugated
deck roof
was soothing
Straining his ears
he could hear
raindrops leapfrogging
through the trees
pelting autumn leaves
as though endeavouring
to persuade them
to let go and move on
Opening his eyes
he watched
a profusion of leaves
descend within the rain
It was as if the sky itself
was falling
He began to feel
cold and dampness
settling in upon him
His eyes drifted
over to the fire pit
A thin wisp of smoke
barely discernable
ascended and disappeared
into the rain-washed gloaming
Was it too late
to rekindle a fire?
Perhaps all there was left

was to close one's eyes
and go to sleep
The notion jostled him
from his reverie
It was a chilling thought
His drink too by this time
had lost all its
warmness and comfort
A slight shiver sent him
shambling over towards
the smouldering fire pit
Stopping by the sea of leaves
he filled his arms
with as much foliage
as possible
Endeavoring to reignite
absent flames
he cast the damp leaves
upon the failing embers
As memories caught fire
a thick grey murky haze
of smoke swirled up
and billowed around him
causing him to tear up
He recoiled from the fire pit
coughing and rubbing his eyes
Standing back
he could clearly perceive
the smoke spiral and curl
up into the forest canopy
Images began to emerge
in the cloudy fumes
Apparitions of lovers
lost

Broken Shells of Memories

abandoned
unrequited
writhed and swirled
in the contorting smoke
He reached out
to no response
They didn't see him
they just drifted off
faded away
leaving him alone
He gazed with envy
and despair upon
the moss-covered rocks
He ached for
a simple connection
one final intimacy
without judgement
or complications
an epiphytic embrace
like a moss embosomed rock

Standing before the window
caught in reflection
What is to be done
with the old tree?
dilapidated and forsaken
limbs once strong
now too old and withered
to be relied on
no longer able to provide
shelter from the elements
not even for itself
Half-eaten and rotting
creaking and complaining
even in the gentlest breeze
The mildew of aspirations
repentantly unfulfilled
stubs and scars laid bare
deadwood, disintegrating leaves
deteriorating memories
desiccated, discarded,
raked, piled, bagged
soon to be carted off
In the waning days
autumn whispers rustle
through offshoots obtruding
irreverently in the background
What is to be done
with the old tree?

About the Author

Craig Gladstone Young was born in East York Township, Ontario Canada in 1957. He spent his childhood and adolescence in Ottawa. Upon graduating from high school he worked in a lumber yard, taking breaks to backpack across Europe and the United Kingdom, then down through the United States, Venezuela and Columbia. He moved to Toronto in 1981, where he worked at a variety of jobs while attending Seneca College. After working for six years in media production, he returned to Ottawa to obtain a degree in Linguistics & Communications at the University of Ottawa. In 1992 he moved to rural Japan to teach English and study martial arts. He met and married his wife Yuki in a Shinto ceremony in the Japanese countryside. In 1999 they returned to Canada where he completed a Bachelor of Education degree. He began a 21 year long career working in high schools, teaching English, Visual Arts, and Media Studies. He currently lives with his wife, two children, and their rescue Jindo-mix pup in Carleton Place, Ontario.

Gladstone

68